Billy Fish

written by Edward S. Popper
illustrated by Jeremy Tugeau

Macmillan
McGraw-Hill

There once lived a boy named Billy Fish. Fish was a good last name for Billy and his parents. They went to the sea often.

Billy had a great talent. He knew how to speak with the sea animals. He could ask a starfish the time of day. He could make a scary shark smile at his jokes.

For Billy's birthday, Mr. and Mrs. Fish took him for a ride on the biggest boat Billy had ever seen.

The boat was like a big, floating party. There were many wonderful things to eat and drink. Everyone was having a good time.

"Some party, isn't it?" the captain asked his guests.

It was some party all right. And some mess!

Cans of juice went flying into the ocean. Bags of chips fell overboard.

Even worse, there was a leak in the boat's engine. The boat left a trail of oil behind it.

Billy was in the middle of a dance when the captain called to him. "Billy, look! It's a blue whale!"

Billy ran to the side of the boat to say hello to the blue whale. But the whale was not in a good mood. He blew oil all over the captain.

The oil missed Billy. It did not miss the captain. Now he was wet and dirty. Oil spotted his nice uniform.

"That awful whale!" the captain cried. "I'll make him pay for this!"

The whale swam away fast.
But more visitors came. Three giant
seahorses swam up to the boat.
Each one had a bag of chips in
its tail. Swaying from side to side,
the seahorses threw the bags
at the guests.

Ick! Soggy chips were everywhere.
Billy and his parents had to duck.

"What's going on?" cried the
captain. "Now these sea animals
have damaged my boat twice!"

Just then, a big head was seen moving toward the boat.

It was an octopus! In each arm, the octopus held three cans of juice!

Plop! Crash! Can after can hit the boat. The boat was covered with sticky juice. The captain was in tears.

"Billy, please!" he cried. "Speak to the octopus!"

"Yes, Billy," said Mr. Fish. "Find out why the animals are acting this way. You're our only chance!" Billy was afraid of the octopus. But he acted bravely.

"Excuse me," he shouted. "Why are you and the whale and the seahorses getting our boat so dirty?"

"We're just giving back what your boat left in our clean ocean," said the octopus. "This is the biggest mess we've ever seen. And it all belongs to you!"

Billy told the captain what the octopus said. "Tell this to your friend," said the captain. "From now on we will keep the ocean clean and safe."

The guests all cheered. Billy gave the biggest cheer of all. The seahorses danced for joy.

Even the octopus waved his arms in the air. All eight of them.